The
Toothbrush Monster

written by Rose Impey
illustrated by Sue Porter

HEINEMANN : LONDON

I don't like to wash my face.
I don't like to comb my hair.
But most of all I hate
to brush my teeth.

My dad says, 'Come here, you mucky monster.'

Sometimes I hide my toothbrush.

'Where is it?' says Dad.

I tell him,
'The Toothbrush Monster stole it.'

'I think you must eat them,'
says Dad.

But I tell him, 'It's not me . . . it's
The Toothbrush Monster.'

My grandad keeps his teeth in
a glass. They grin at me.
'Snap! Snap! Look out! They bite,'
says Grandad.

I'd like to keep my teeth in a glass.
I wiggle them every night.
But they won't come out.

At bedtime Grandad says, 'Open up.
Who's going to do them, you or me?'

So I say . . .
'The Toothbrush Monster.'